JUST BEFORE DAWN

Also by Jan Mogensen

Mary's Christmas Present
Ted and the Chinese Princess
Lost and Found
Ted's Seaside Adventure
Ted Runs Away from Home

HAMISH HAMILTON CHILDREN'S BOOKS

Penguin Books Ltd, 27 Wrights Lane, London W8 5TZ (Publishing & Editorial)
and Harmondsworth, Middlesex, England (Distribution & Warehouse)
Viking Penguin Inc., 40 West 23rd Street, New York, New York 10010, U.S.A
Penguin Books Australia Ltd, Ringwood, Victoria, Australia
Penguin Books Canada Limited, 2801 John Street, Markham, Ontario, Canada L3R 1B4
Penguin Books (N.Z) Ltd, 182-190 Wairau Road, Auckland 10, New Zealand

First published in Great Britain 1982 by
Hamish Hamilton Children's Books

Copyright © 1981 Jan Mogensen

English text copyright © 1982 Hamish Hamilton Ltd.

Reprinted 1987

Published by arrangement with Borgen, Copenhagen

British Library Cataloguing in Publication Data

Mogensen, Jan
Just before dawn
I. Title
839.8'1374 [J] PZ7
ISBN 0-241-10719-9

Typeset by Katerprint Co. Ltd, Oxford
Printed in Denmark

JAN MOGENSEN

JUST BEFORE DAWN

English text by
WENDY WOLF

Hamish Hamilton · London

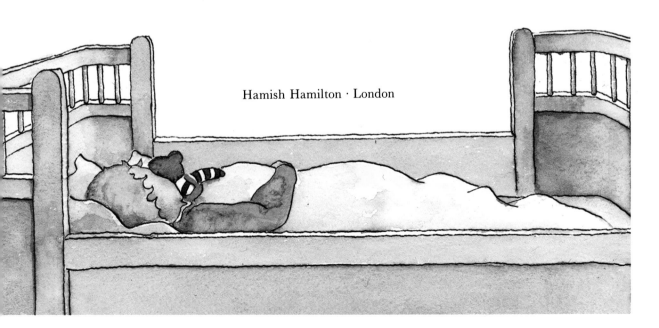

Early one summer morning just before dawn, while Jim was still asleep, Teddy woke up. He was restless and turned from side to side. But no matter what he did he couldn't go back to sleep. He stared around him wide awake. I shall get up and try on the Punch puppet's hat, he thought.

Teddy took the hat and tried it on. It felt
good. Then he saw the drum. He took it down
and slipped the cord over his head. The first
pale rays of the sun appeared behind the
houses as Teddy climbed down to the window
sill to play. It was like a stage, so he marched
backwards and forwards banging on the
drum. Teddy was so happy that he did not
notice that the window was open.

Suddenly Teddy stumbled, and lost his footing on the sill. He fell backwards out through the bars of the window into the still morning air outside.

Teddy tumbled down and down into the yard below. He saw the hat and the drum vanish into the shadows. Then with a bump he landed on something soft and black.

In the yard beside the house it was still dark, but Teddy saw that he had fallen onto the garden cat who slept in the yard.

"Whatever are you doing?" snapped the startled cat.

Teddy felt foolish and said,

"I fell from the window while I was playing with my drum, but it is so far away that I don't know how I shall get back." The cat looked up at the window.

"I cannot jump that high but I could take you as far as the shed roof."

"Oh thank you," said Teddy.

Garden cat leapt onto the bicycle shed, and along the fence, with Teddy dizzily clinging to his back. Beneath the fence stood an open dustbin.

"Take care that we don't fall in there," whispered Teddy into the cat's fur. "Nonsense," said the cat, and together they sailed up onto the roof of the big shed.

"Now you will have to manage the rest of the way on your own. I cannot take you any farther."

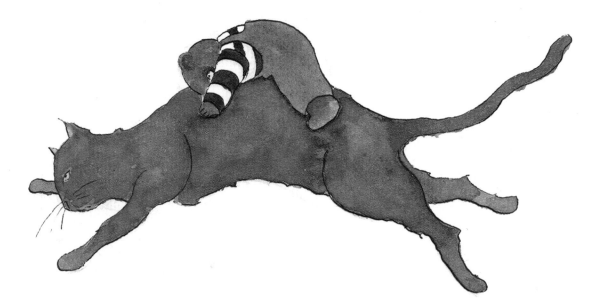

Before Teddy could thank him again, the cat had gone.

Teddy looked up at the open window and
wondered what to do. He felt all alone. Soon
Jim will wake up and miss me, and he will be
very sorry that I am not there with him. The
thought was so sad that Teddy sat down and
cried.

Suddenly Teddy heard a voice.

"Whatever are you crying for?"

He turned round in surprise and saw two squirrels in the tree.

"I want to go back to my home. I slipped and fell while I was playing. Garden cat carried me here but I cannot go any farther."

Big tears ran down his cheeks as he pointed up to the open window. The squirrels followed the direction in which Teddy pointed.

"We could get you through the tree and onto the telegraph pole, and then you would have to manage the rest of the way on your own."

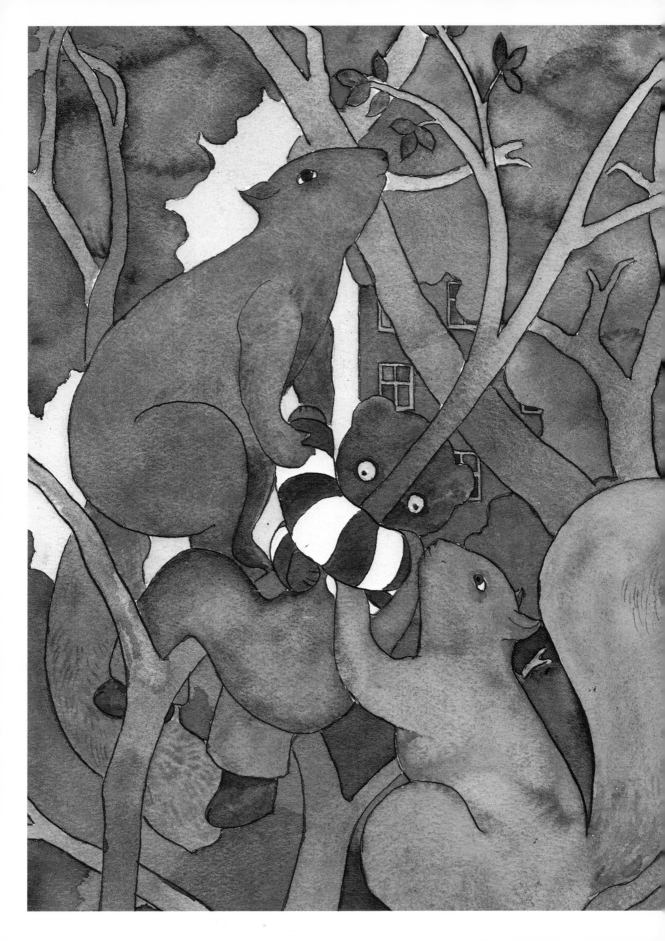

The two squirrels pushed Teddy up into the tree. Once inside he found the darkness frightening. The squirrels helped him up through the branches, and all the while the leaves rustled and fluttered.

"I do hope there are no ghosts," he said.

But the squirrels did not know what ghosts were, and so they said nothing. At last they reached the telegraph pole.

The darkness of the tree had been frightening, but now Teddy was all alone on top of the pole. The squirrels jumped back into the tree and waved goodbye. "Good luck," they said, and they disappeared just as the cat had done.

"Hey wait," shouted Teddy. "I don't want to stay here alone." But his words were blown away.

A wire stretched from the pole to the house, almost to the open window. If I could cross that, Teddy thought, I would be almost home. But it is a long way, and very dangerous. What if I slipped again? Then he remembered Jim. If he wakes up and sees that I am gone, he will be so sad.

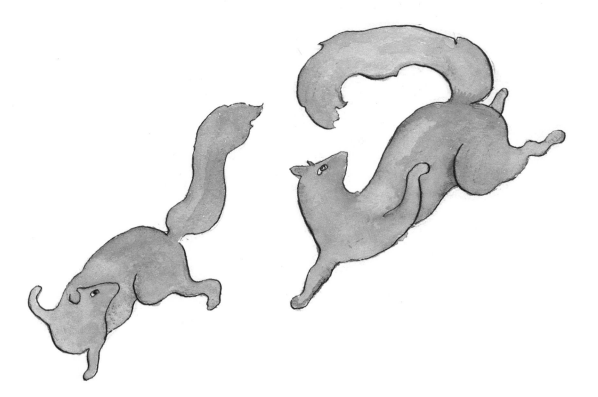

Teddy stepped out onto the wire. He carefully placed one foot in front of the other, and took some rapid steps forward. He tried not to look down at the yard so far below. But then he lost his balance and the yard seemed to swing up at him. He stopped and waited until he was ready and then began to cross again.

Just as Teddy reached the wire near to the window his foot slipped and he fell. At that moment a pigeon flew by, and he dived to save Teddy. Grasping him firmly by his trousers, the pigeon carried him towards the open window.

Gently the pigeon placed Teddy on the
window ledge. "What a good thing I flew by
when I did!"

"Yes," said Teddy. "I cannot tell you how
happy I am to be home." He hugged the
pigeon fondly, and tears of joy ran down his
cheeks and onto the pigeon's feathers.

Teddy watched and waved as the pigeon
flew away towards the sun, over the roof tops
and out of sight. Then he hurried into the
room where Jim lay still asleep.

At the very moment Teddy lay down once
more on the bed, Jim opened his eyes.
Turning towards Teddy he said "Good
morning, Teddy, did you sleep well?"
But Teddy did not reply. He simply smiled.